Adventures of
Strawberry
Shortcake

Penguin Young Readers
An Imprint of Penguin Group (USA) Inc.

PENGUIN YOUNG READERS
An Imprint of Penguin Random House LLC

ISBN 9781101950180

10 9 8 7 6 5 4 3 2

Table of Contents

We Love You,
Strawberry Shortcake!

by Sierra Harimann
illustrated by Marci Beighley

Strawberry Shortcake

is a berry sweet girl.

She likes to show
her friends how much
she cares about them.

Strawberry's friends like
to show they care, too.

Plum Pudding has an idea.

Everyone can give

Strawberry a gift.

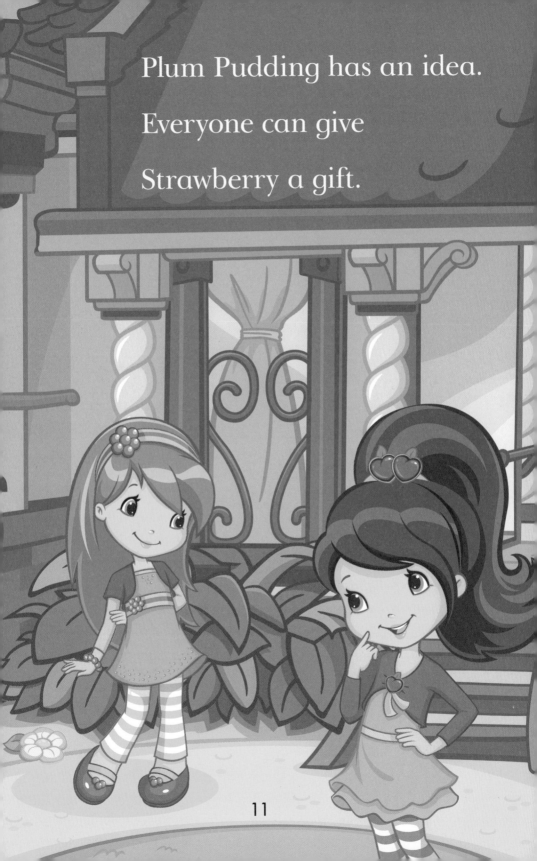

Raspberry Torte wants to throw

Strawberry a surprise party.

Both ideas are good.

The girls will have a party

and bring gifts!

Plum and Raspberry

know what to give Strawberry.

So do Lemon Meringue

and Blueberry Muffin.

Orange Blossom does not
know what to give Strawberry.
But then she gets an idea!

15

Strawberry's friends
set up for the party.
It will be berry fun!

We Love You, Strawberry!

17

It is almost party time.

Blueberry calls Strawberry.

She asks Strawberry

to come to the bookstore.

Strawberry says she will

come right away.

Strawberry opens the door.

What a surprise!

Lemon pours lemonade.

Raspberry serves fruit salad.

21

Plum is the first to give

Strawberry a gift.

It is a dance lesson!

23

Next, Blueberry
gives her gift
to Strawberry.

It is a book for

Strawberry's recipes.

26

Then, Lemon gives

her gift to Strawberry.

It is a haircut.

Next, Strawberry opens
a box from Raspberry.
Inside is a pretty,
new dress!

Orange feels very sad.

Her gift is not

like the other gifts.

Orange tells Strawberry
her gift was just
going to be a hug.

Strawberry thinks a hug

is a perfect gift!

Strawberry says,
"Thank you."
She loves her party
and all her gifts.

But Strawberry loves
her berry best friends
even more!

Ballet School

by Sierra Harimann
illustrated by Lisa Workman

Strawberry Shortcake
and her friends are going
to dance class.

Plum Pudding is the teacher.

The girls are ready.

It is time to dance!

The music starts.

The girls move to the beat.

Up and down.

Up and down.

Next, the girls put

their hands on their hips.

Then they point their toes.

Tap, tap, tap.

A new song starts.

The girls skip across the room.

Skip, skip, skip, skip.

One, two, three, four.

Now it is time to leap.

Blueberry Muffin

and Strawberry go first.

They leap berry high.

Next, Lemon Meringue leaps.

Lemon wishes she could

leap higher.

Orange Blossom leaps.

Raspberry Torte leaps, too.

Lemon is not having fun.

Plum asks Lemon why she is sad.

Lemon says she is

not good at ballet.

Lemon's friends tell her

she is good at lots of things.

Orange says Lemon

is a good friend.

Strawberry says Lemon

makes the best hair braids.

Raspberry says Lemon

is a berry good listener.

But Lemon is still sad.

Plum tells Lemon

she can be good at ballet, too.

She just has to practice,

try her berry best,

and have fun!

Next, the girls do spins.

But Lemon is having trouble.

Lemon tries another spin.

This time, she does better.

Lemon is doing her best.

She is having a good time!

Everyone thanks Plum

for a great ballet class.

It was berry, berry fun!

Strawberry Shortcake™

Lost and Found

by Lana Jacobs
illustrated by MJ Illustrations

The sun is out.

Strawberry Shortcake plays

with her friends.

69

70

Her pets play, too.

Pupcake is her dog.

Custard is her cat.

71

Look!

It is starting to rain.

The girls run inside.

It is dry inside.

Oh no!

Where are Pupcake

and Custard?

Strawberry will look for them.

Her friends want to help.

Strawberry puts on her raincoat
and rain boots.

Don't forget the umbrellas!

Strawberry and her friends

go to the shop.

Pupcake and Custard

are not at the shop.

84

Strawberry and her friends
go to town.

Pupcake and Custard
are not in town.

Strawberry is sad.

Will she ever find

Pupcake and Custard?

Look!

Cat and dog

paw prints!

The girls follow
the paw prints
to a flower patch.

Look!

Pupcake and Custard

are taking a nap.

Strawberry is happy.

Now it is time to go home.

The rain has stopped.

Look!

A rainbow is in the sky!

It is a happy end to the day.

A Picnic Adventure

by Lisa Gallo
illustrated by Laura Thomas

It is berry nice outside!

Strawberry Shortcake
and her friends will
go on a hike.

Blueberry Muffin
tells her friends about
Berry Bitty Falls.

They can have

a picnic there!

The girls pack

a yummy lunch.

Blueberry takes a map.

Orange Blossom brings a camera.

On the hike, Lemon Meringue

sees a rosebush.

Orange takes a photo.

Say cheese!

Look!

A cool stream.

Orange takes a photo.

Click!

Strawberry picks up

some rocks.

Then, Plum Pudding

sees a bird's nest.

Orange takes a photo.

Blueberry looks at the map.

They are berry close
to the waterfall!

They find the waterfall!

It is berry pretty!

The girls sit down.

They have a picnic.

Now it is time to go home.

They take one last photo.

Oh no!

The map blew away!

Blueberry is scared.

How will they get home

without the map?

Strawberry has an idea!

They will get home

if they find the nest,

the stream, and the roses.

Where is the bird's nest?

There it is!

Where is the stream?

There it is!

The girls are going the right way.

Hooray!

Where is the rosebush?

There it is!

The girls are almost home!

Look, the café!

They made it home.

What a great day!